The Edge

Paul Symonloe

TSL Drama

Dedication

To my long-suffering Confidant

~ ~

Cast list

Michael: Man in his late 20s wearing a close-fitting suit. Serious and practical.

Daphné: Poised, fiery French woman in her mid-20s. Attractive, smartly dressed and business-like. Completely bilingual with a very slight [but detectable] French accent. Not coquettish.

Mungo: Businessman of a little over 50.

Raj: Asian man of around 60.

Stephen: Man in his late 50s. Raffish in appearance.

Youth: Youth of 18 or so.

Policewoman: Young, efficient.

Running Time
90 minutes

ACT 1 SCENE 1

Setting:

To one side of the stage is part of a bridge, the rest having collapsed. On the other side is the bumper of a car, the rest being off-stage. In the far distance we hear sirens, while on-stage are two figures. One is a woman, DAPHNÉ, of around twenty-five, the other a man, MICHAEL, nearly thirty. They are both talking excitedly on their mobiles, occasionally looking at each other in a – rather overly – disinterested way, suggesting they are strangers. We are aware of distant thunder and lightning.

DAPHNÉ: [*on mobile*] It disappeared just like that! Jesus, ten seconds earlier and I'd be fucking dead right now! [*Sits down shocked on the bonnet of the car*] Yes, yes of course I will. It's just the shock, I'll be okay.

MICHAEL: [*on the other side of the stage on his mobile*] I'm telling you it's completely gone! I can't get back until someone comes up here. [*pauses for a reply*] No, no it's totally backed up, no one can move in either direction. The road narrows at the bridge and there's no space to turn round. Plus I think the way I came must be completely flooded too. There's no going back. [*pauses for a reply*] No! The water just took over! Helen listen is Sean okay? Did the school say anything about you know what? [*pauses for a reply*] Okay, yes I'll call you again when something happens. [*ends call*]

DAPHNÉ: [*still on mobile*] No, it's gone quiet now. I don't know else at the moment. I'll call you as soon as I do. [*pauses for a reply*] Yes, me too, bye.

[*The two strangers, DAPHNÉ and MICHAEL, look across at each other tentatively, not knowing whether to speak or not. DAPHNÉ sits on the bonnet of the car again, leading us to think it's probably hers. They keep looking at each other and then looking away, waiting for the other to speak. Eventually the man opens the dialogue.*]

MICHAEL: [*showing concern*] Hi there, I'm Michael. You okay?

DAPHNÉ: [*sightly ironic, with feeling*] Yeah! I nearly died! Christ this is shit! [*smiles*] Daphné, hi.

MICHAEL: What happened? You were right at the front right?

DAPHNÉ: Yes, I was the last one before it all fell apart. You know what's awful, I think a car could have gone over the edge. I'm not sure, because I couldn't see really with the rain and the river going crazy! Oh my god! If someone fell in people could be dead, couldn't they?

MICHAEL: Jesus! Is that what happened?

DAPHNÉ: [*not committing*] Well, I don't know for sure. I'm not swearing to it. As I said, the rain was like a wall of water. I couldn't see a thing. I think I stopped my car out of instinct. Where are you?

MICHAEL: I'm five back. A guy in the car behind you went to sit in the white van right behind him. Maybe they know each other.

DAPHNÉ: [*looks sceptical*] Is there any evidence for that? Three cars in a convoy you mean? Sounds pretty unlikely.

MICHAEL: [*less sure*] Okay, perhaps not, but as I say he went to sit in the white van. I expect he wanted company, reassurance, that kind of thing.

DAPHNÉ: [*unconvinced*] Maybe. Did you notice anyone else?

MICHAEL: No, I was so freaked out by the bridge going down too, I didn't notice anything else. Maybe the police will tell us more.

DAPHNÉ: [*a little challenging*] So, you've called them?

MICHAEL: No, no I haven't. I thought someone would've done by now.

DAPHNÉ: [*business-like*] So you haven't and assumed someone else would?

MICHAEL: [*simply*] Yes.

DAPHNÉ: [*energetic, not scolding*] So, I'm going to! Somebody has to act, right? [*she punches the numbers decisively into her mobile*] Merde! I think I'm in France! [*starts again*] It's the shock.

MICHAEL: Don't worry, nobody's around to hear you, we're cut off.

DAPHNÉ: [*factually*] You're here. Anyway I don't like being cut off – story of my life. Wait, they're answering now. [*she walks off towards the bridge leaving the man and the audience excluded from what she is saying. Every so often she gestures towards the collapsed bridge, to the water, and in the direction of the stationary cars. Ends call and returns to the man's side*]

Okay, so they know about it, but have no idea when they'll be able to send help. They say we might want to keep out of our vehicles 'in case of inundation'. But it's up to us. [*suddenly angry*] Bloody hell, I was supposed to be doing something tonight!

MICHAEL: [*triggered by her temperament*] Me too as it happens! My boss was coming over to go through some figures. What a kerfuffle!

DAPHNÉ: [*suddenly amused*] What a kerfuffle!? Not a disaster? Just a little local difficulty right? You English!

MICHAEL: [*with dignity*] Yes, I'm English. Is that okay?

DAPHNÉ: [still *amused*] Of course it's okay! We're in England aren't we?

MICHAEL: Yes we are … [*tails off*]

DAPHNÉ: [*looks at him appraisingly*] Do you think I'm having a go at you? [MICHAEL *doesn't respond*] Well I'm not. Differences are good. They can be the lightning between us right? A connection in a storm! You react this way, I that. It's interesting, [*not coquettish*] exciting even.

MICHAEL:	[*ironic*]. This weather is damned exciting! It's getting more exciting every year.
DAPHNÉ:	Yes, it's insanity! Are we going to wake up?
MICHAEL:	The climate thing you mean?
DAPHNÉ:	[*incredulous*] Climate thing?! Yes! The climate thing! How long have we got left, thirty years, fifty?
MICHAEL:	[*pause as he observes her temperament. Enter an Asian man of around 60, vocally relieved to see them*]
RAJ:	Thanks to God! Are both of you alright? Do you know if anyone went over the edge? What a catastrophe! Oh goodness, I'm so glad you're both alive! Would you like some sandwiches? I'm in the van up here with a woman and a man. Come, come I'll give you food. I've got Fanta too.
	[*the two younger adults look at each other for guidance,* DAPHNÉ *reacts first*]
DAPHNÉ:	That's very kind of you Mr...
RAJ:	Raj, just Raj. Please come, come.
MICHAEL:	Thanks, but I reckon I'll stay here and keep an eye open for the emergency services. This is a good vantage point.
RAJ:	Please, what is your name?
MICHAEL:	Michael.
RAJ:	Please Mr Michael, come with us. It's probably going to rain again soon and just here is perhaps not safe. The ground is too soft and it can give way. Please you come and Miss...
DAPHNÉ:	Daphné
RAJ:	... Miss Daphné. Come to my van to eat and drink.
	[MICHAEL *considers*]
MICHAEL:	Okay, look I've just got a couple of calls to make, and then I'll come over. Which van is it?
RAJ:	It is the only van. Come soon please. Miss Daphne,

come with me please.

[*They leave.* MICHAEL *dials and puts the mobile to his ear*]

MICHAEL: Hi. [*pause for reply*] No, don't worry, I'm fine. Is this on the news by the way? [*pause*] Shit! Really? [*with growing emphasis*] Really?! So half the county's under water? Jesus! Okay, it looks like it'll be a long night then. Sean's okay, right? Yes I know. Okay, tell him I'll be home soon. [*longish pause*] Are you serious Helen? Tonight of all nights? I'm up to my ears in flood-water and you're going out? Who's going to look after Sean? [*pause*] Your mother? I thought you said she wasn't well? [*pause, angry*] Right, well there's nothing I can do about it is there? Look I have to go. [*rings off abruptly, dials again*]

Hi Nick? [*pause*] Yes it's me again. [*pause*] ... In some kind of trouble? You don't know the half of it. No I'm on the B1077 near Little Millbridge. The old bridge went down in a flood. We're marooned on a single track road. [*pause*] ... No it's stopped raining for now. [*pause*] Yes I just called her. [*pause*] Oh she's fine. She says she's going out tonight and leaving Sean with her sick mother, would you believe?! [*pause*] Yes, that is the kind of person she is! [*pause*] Christ what a fuckup this all is. Listen, there's someone coming. Can you call me back in five Nick? Great, thanks. [*ends call*]

[RAJ *returns with a pack of sandwiches and a can of Fanta*]

RAJ: Mr Michael, I want you to have these to eat and drink please.

[MICHAEL *looks slightly guilty and takes the offerings with a genuine smile*]

MICHAEL: Look I'm sorry I haven't come over. I've got a health issue with my son. He needs round-the-clock atten-tion and it turns out my wife's going out. Anyway, it's

	very good of you to think of me. Thanks so much for these. [*holds up sandwiches*]
RAJ:	Actually you are quite welcome. I'm sorry to hear about your son. How old is he? Is his mother going to leave him alone for long?
MICHAEL:	[*shocked*] Oh heavens no, we'd never leave him on his own. His grandmother will be there to look after him. He's only seven.
RAJ:	You don't trust her, your wife's mother?
MICHAEL:	[*again eager to be clear*] No, no, it's not that. She's elderly and not too well either, that's all.
RAJ:	If she's quite ill herself, she should not be in charge. Do you wish me to ask my own mother to go there?
MICHAEL:	[*still slightly shocked*] No really, that's very kind but it's fine. I'm going to ask a friend of mine to check on him later. He needs his medication.
RAJ:	You think that he can die? [MICHAEL *looks uncomfortable at this comment, turns away*] I see you don't like to think about death. I'm sorry. Mine is a different background, sometimes you have to think about it. Look at tonight for example. Miss Daphné came very close to her death, really close. Maybe some people did die on that bridge. We have to wait patiently to find out.
MICHAEL:	[*mobile starts ringing, putting it to his ear gestures he's got to take the call. Looks apologetic. RAJ leaves*] Nick? [*pause*] Thanks for calling back. Look can you do me a big favour? [*pause*] Yes, you guessed. Do you mind? I'd be really grateful. [*pause*] God, thanks, I owe you. [*ends call and puts his hands through his hair, then covers his face. After some seconds in this position he looks up to find* DAPHNÉ *next to him. He straightens up*]
DAPHNÉ:	You okay? Michael, right?
MICHAEL:	Yes, Michael.

DAPHNÉ:	I'm guessing there's something wrong?
MICHAEL:	No, no... [*relenting*] well yes, I suppose. I was just saying to that guy Raj, I'm worried about my son's health. The medics can't pin down the problem. Not being able to be with him... [*tails off*]
DAPHNÉ:	[*sympathetic*] It sucks right?
MICHAEL:	Yes.
DAPHNÉ:	Look, why don't you come over to the van. There's a kind of weird guy there with Raj. Maybe it would take your mind off things?
MICHAEL:	Weird guy?
DAPHNÉ:	Yes. He's in to a 1960's look, longish hair and a flowery shirt, that kind of thing, quite attractive in an out-dated way. [*laughs*] Anyway come with me. It'll help, trust me.
MICHAEL:	[*not convinced*]. Actually I think I'll play it safe. Didn't the police say it may be dangerous to be inside our vehicles? It may start coming down again. The hills can dump half a river on you without warning.
DAPHNÉ:	[jokily] Do you always play it safe Michael? They said it may be dangerous to be outside our vehicles too. [*smiles, seeing he's decided*] Okay, but I won't be saving your skin if it all goes wrong. [*makes to go*]
MICHAEL:	Thanks for asking though [*experimentally*] Daphné.
DAPHNÉ:	[*lightly, friendly*] No worries.
MICHAEL:	[*jokily*] Okay I'll be over in a couple of ... days!
DAPHNÉ:	[*laughs*] Sure. Don't get tempted by the river will you? Some people get a fatal fascination like that, and the next thing you know ... [*she whistles a downward cadence suggesting a fall*]
MICHAEL:	Don't worry I've got too many responsibilities. [*sudden smile*] Anyway, I'm a coward!
DAPHNÉ:	[*laughs*] Pleased to hear it! Loyalty to cowardice is still loyalty right? See you later. [*exits. MICHAEL goes*

	over to the bank, studies the running. He spends quite some time close to the edge. STEPHEN *enters, approaches*]
STEPHEN:	Man! Quite a spectacle right? A dreadful abyss with artistic possibilities! I should take some pictures, except you can't capture a sense of destruction or an undercurrent of chaos on a roll of film.
MICHAEL:	[*friendly*] Hi, Michael. [*offers a hand*]
STEPHEN:	[*shakes*] Stephen, ciao. I've been in the van with Raj, and later with an attractive French woman, Daphné? Are you two friends?
MICHAEL:	No. I was close behind when the bridge went down that's all. She was at the front. I guess she's already told you?
STEPHEN:	She has. It must have been horrific. She must have thought she was going to die. [*smiles, oddly out of keeping with the topic*] She seems completely together though. I reckon she's not easily fazed. You can tell by the way she talks and stands – body language – I notice stuff like that.
MICHAEL:	[*looks frankly at the other man*] Right. You seem pretty un-fazed yourself. Have you got any more news on this mess?
STEPHEN:	[*ignores the question*] I'm on a natural high. Besides, I've looked in to any number of chasms. We're helpless as babies out here you know? Shall we cross the Acheron covering our ears to the screams of the Uncommitted?
MICHAEL:	[*puzzled*] Sorry, I don't know what you're talking about.
STEPHEN:	Sorry. I'm being obscure. It's Dante's *Inferno*. This bridge and the angry waters remind me of his journey across the river Acheron, hearing the tormented screams of those who chose neither side in life – not good or evil – thinking only of themselves.

MICHAEL: Right! Cheerful!

STEPHEN: Yes, 'abandon hope all ye who enter here' and all
              that jazz. It isn't exactly a bedtime story is it? Any-
              way, what's yours?

MICHAEL: My what?

STEPHEN: Your story? Everyone's got a story. It's funny how
              being thrown together like this makes you open up.

MICHAEL: [*stiffly*] I'm not sure I am opening up.

STEPHEN: You will, if we're here long enough, believe me. Once
              the rat's maze of people's minds gets going. It should
              be interesting.

MICHAEL: Interesting?

STEPHEN: Sure.

MICHAEL: Sounds like a human experiment.

STEPHEN: Maybe. With people there's always subtext, a back-
              story. What happens if I do this or that? As long as
              we're trapped here, an experiment of some kind is
              inescapable.

              [*They're interrupted by* DAPHNÉ *returning. She in turn
              looks round hearing a voice, seeing she's been fol-
              lowed on to the stage by* MUNGO. *He's just ending a
              call to the police. Broadcasts*]

MUNGO: You won't believe the breaking news! There's a dam
              up on that ridge, [*points*] by the name of Tall Water,
              straining like a woman with sextuplets, to drop a mil-
              lion tons of water on our heads!

MICHAEL: [*alarmed*] What?! What the hell are the police doing
              about getting us out?!

MUNGO: [*issues his response generally, not an answer to*
              MICHAEL] The police say they've escorted most of
              the stranded drivers to safety back along the main
              road as far as the cutting. However, as of now, it's
              been deemed unsafe because of the ceaseless rain,
              hence we [*makes a circular motion with his finger*]

	are stuck here! That is until they pronounce it safe again or find another way of saving our skins!
DAPHNÉ:	So, we're just to sit here and wait to be swept away?
STEPHEN:	Marvellous! A cliff-hanger. The thrill of waiting to see what happens next.
MICHAEL:	It's no thrill for me thanks! Look, I'll call the police again. [*puts his mobile to his ear, pause, and looks round at the others*] Shit! No signal!
	[RAJ *enters. He seems excited to see* MUNGO]
RAJ:	There you are Mr Mungo. Please have some sandwiches. [*offers a pack*]
MUNGO:	Look, I've told you once I don't eat sandwiches!
RAJ:	[*philosophical*] Okay Mr Mungo, just let me know when you change your mind. Every person must eat.
MUNGO:	[*looks around, sarcastic*] Maybe you can trade them with someone else.
RAJ:	No, no I am not selling them, although they are one of our best lines, I have to admit. Out here in this very bad storm they are for us all to share. We are all human people caught together in a difficult situation.
DAPHNÉ:	Thank you Raj, I enjoyed mine. [*meaningfully to* MUNGO] At least someone's thinking of others.
MICHAEL:	Yes, good on you Raj.
STEPHEN:	[*facetious*] Yes, you may have a bit-part at the moment Raj, but it has distinct promise if we're stuck here without food for days.
MICHAEL:	[*piqued*] I don't see the joke. We're cut off in the cold and dark. What's sure is that we'll need each other.
MUNGO:	[*looks at him appraisingly, sceptical*] I can't say I know what you mean. As things stand I'm simply stuck on the road to nowhere with a few other specimens of humanity. When help arrives, that's it!

RUTH:	That's never it. Why do you talk as though you're the only one who counts?
MUNGO:	Do I? Well, let me clarify, I have no horse in this race. I'll be out of here shortly and shall, without intending offence, forget you all instantly.
DAPHNÉ:	Without intending offence? You seem very sure you won't need anyone out here in the dark.
MUNGO:	[dry] It isn't actually dark yet. Anyway, must I supress what I say to 'keep in' with you all? Am I to choose my words from a menu?
DAPHNÉ:	No, but it's probably unintelligent to ignore the facts.
MUNGO:	Which are?
DAPHNÉ:	That we may be in danger, and if so, relationships count. [glares at him] Like family ties, if you have one that is.
MUNGO:	[faces her down]. You're very young aren't you? Do you really view this assemblage as your saviours? Seems your geese are all swans.
DAPHNE:	So I shouldn't see the good in people?
MUNGO:	We all think that way at first, seeing the best in people. If I can offer a little fatherly advice, you should start making smart choices.
DAPHNÉ:	Such as?
MUNGO:	Such as searching out those who've made their mark in the world.
MICHAEL:	Bullies perhaps?
MUNGO:	Winners perhaps.
STEPHEN:	[grinning, at MUNGO] Talking of winners, is your car the Range Rover by any chance?
MUNGO:	[dry] Yes, why?
STEPHEN:	Oh nothing, just asking.
MUNGO:	There's a motive behind all questions.
DAPHNÉ:	A sad view.

MUNGO:	Actually not. It's human nature. We're all in it for ourselves. If this guy asks me about my car it's because either he's jealous or he's got one.
DAPHNÉ:	What if he's just making conversation?
MUNGO:	Words matter, even to a clown. [*turns to* STEPHEN] Okay, so tell us, why did you ask the question?
STEPHEN:	[*not insulted*] I'm just interested in people's choices. I reckon you see an expensive car as an ingredient in your worth to the world.
MUNGO:	And my number plates?
STEPHEN:	Those are your footprints in the sand.
MUNGO:	Based on what theory?
STEPHEN:	[*grins*] That they make you appear more attractive than your personal skills suggest.
MUNGO:	[*dismissive*] Plates like mine are common enough. That sounds like a lame theory to me. You're big on observation, but what have you ever done?
STEPHEN:	Neatly proving my point that you confuse wealth with worth. I don't need a number-plate to justify myself.
DAPHNÉ:	[*jumping in*] Damn the number plate! Time's against us here. The road's unstable and where is the help they promised?
STEPHEN:	[*hurriedly*] She's right. We are in a spot of bother. The dam over that hill must be bursting. It's getting late. What is it ...? [*looks at his phone*] 8 p.m.? The light's going and it's getting cold. We don't know if sitting in our cars is safe. Like the sea-farers in the *Tempest*, salvaged but muddled.
MUNGO:	[*knowledgeable, dry*] However our storm, we assume, wasn't summoned up by magic. Moreover, if this is a story of sibling rivalry and betrayal we may all be in danger. Maybe we should ask if we're in acceptable company? [*sarcastic*] Except of course that

we have no choice regarding the company, do we?

DAPHNÉ: You do. You can choose to avoid us.

MICHAEL: [*also irritated*] I don't know which nuthouse you've all escaped from but can we just focus?

STEPHEN: Okay, let's each put forward a plan to get us out of here. Maybe give some background on who we are, and any relevant skills. [*smiles*] It could be life or death.

DAPHNÉ: [*incredulous*] Life or death? That's just nuts! We're just waiting for the emergency services to arrive? Why the drama?

STEPHEN: Okay, no drama, but I think we should know more about each other. Anyway, it'll help pass the time until someone comes.

RAJ: Actually, I think Mr Stephen is right in this particular matter. We should all listen respectfully to each person. Maybe say who we are and what we can do to help.

MICHAEL: Okay, I'm with Raj. I'll suggest a plan, but help may arrive in an hour or two.

DAPHNÉ: Or ten. We can't exactly check-out any time we like can we?

STEPHEN: Brilliant! A Hotel California clause!

MUNGO: On just that theme, [*to* STEPHEN] if the spirit of sixty-nine over here thinks we're as good as shipwrecked on an island of magic and mischief, maybe we should get on with going through the runners and riders.

STEPHEN: [*laughing, flippant*] Okay, right. Who are we all then and what are our combined skills?

DAPHNÉ: [*to* STEPHEN] Okay you start. Who are you?

STEPHEN: [*still flippant*] I would say, but who I am kind of depends on who you all are. Why don't we find out who we want the others to think we are?

MICHAEL: [*annoyed*] Jesus Christ! Look, I'll share my ideas but I'm not going in to detail about myself.

MUNGO: [*mock surprise*] No? Well the devil's in the detail, they say.

MICHAEL: [*enigmatic*] You bet.

MUNGO: [*changing tone*] Actually one need only engage in this 'show and tell' if one wishes. In this instance I choose to because it makes sense. Maybe [*looking around*] someone can start and we can get this out of the way? [*to MICHAEL*] Maybe you have a tale to tell?

MICHAEL: [*dry*]. Maybe we all do.

MUNGO: [*impatient*] For Christ's sake! [*to STEPHEN*] It was your idea, perhaps you can get on with it!

STEPHEN: [*smiling, arch*] You know your temper may be your downfall.

MUNGO: And flippancy may be yours.

DAPHNÉ: [*to MUNGO*] I really don't know who you are, or your name come to that, but hasn't anyone ever told you you're bloody rude?

MUNGO: [*Simply*] Yes, and it's Mungo.

DAPHNÉ: You're a bit thin on friends I guess, Mungo?

MUNGO: I don't consider making friends paramount actually, and since I'm already speaking, I'll say what I would do in this situation.

STEPHEN: Hallelujah!

MUNGO: I'm Mungo De Fren. I don't have a huge number of friends as we've just established …

STEPHEN: [*sarcastic*] Really?

MUNGO: [*not distracted*] … But I'm true to myself, if that's a measure of anything, which perhaps it is. I don't consider being nice hugely useful.

MICHAEL: [*quietly*] You can say that again.

MUNGO:	[*ignoring him*] Invariably people are nice to win favour and so advance their own lives. I'm Oxford-educated and have worked in finance most of my life. I like to see things as they are. I feel my job should be to challenge any ideas or plans put forward. I'll be an adjudicator. [*signals with a finger to his throat he's finished his story*]
STEPHEN:	And a truly modest one.
DAPHNÉ:	[*business-like*] Okay, I'll go next. I'm Daphné and [*looking at MUNGO*] I hope I'm different from this guy.
MUNGO:	Mungo.
DAPHNÉ:	[*ignoring him*] I think my skills are balancing out one risk against another. I'm a lawyer. I work on testaments and inheritance between the English and French legal systems.
STEPHEN:	Great! Huge scope for familial intrigues!
DAPHNÉ:	[*coolly*] It's most dull, actually but I see into the lives of the bereaved. Death brings out the basic good in people and the opposite, of course. Often an acid test of a person's humanity. [*looks at MUNGO*]
MUNGO:	[*Reacting*] Forgive me, are you suggesting that my not being overly nice to people makes me a bad person? Maybe you think, going on this hippy's plotline, I'm some kind of erratic monster?
DAPHNÉ:	Monster is too loaded, but you clearly have a knack for offending people. Why refer to him as a hippy? Can't you just ask his name?
STEPHEN:	Hey, I downed the cup of love and peace. I'm okay with it.
MUNGO:	[*ignoring him*] And why exactly would the term hippy be offensive? He dresses like one and I'm quite sure his look is entirely intentional. I see things as they are, that's all. I see no negatives here.
STEPHEN:	Nor me. I'm still spangling in the afterglow.

DAPHNÉ:	[*to* MUNGO] No, but you understand the power of words. You claim to see things as they are, but it's all subjective. You see things one way and I another. The truth may lie anywhere in between, or we may both be totally wrong.
MUNGO:	So it's subjective; that's true for everyone.
DAPHNÉ:	Yes, and we should be challenged for it, especially for under-the-radar prejudice, our prejudice 'software'.
MUNGO:	Software?
DAPHNÉ:	Yes. The thinking we start life with, our default. How many of us walk well clear of beggars, privately wishing they'd disappear? They make us feel uncomfortable, as do people with mental problems. We edge away.
MUNGO:	Okay. What about the youth of today, despising us illogically for trashing the planet and their future?
DAPHNÉ:	And you can't see their point?
MUNGO:	I can't, or not enough to lay charges against everyone who came before. Try second-guessing what your children will blame you for. That's a so-called software prejudice.
DAPHNÉ:	But your generation had a choice. Your default with the young is their lack of experience.
MUNGO:	Perhaps.
DAPHNÉ:	You view them as unable to see the full picture. You argue they can't possibly know. But giving the lie to that is over there! [*points to the river*] That's what they know; a disaster in real time.
MUNGO:	And you think we conspired to destroy the planet and have all life perish? There were two wars remember? Nobody was even aware of the science. Plus we have to believe the science. Just what would your generation have done differently?

DAPHNÉ: [*avoiding*] To conclude, I have a boyfriend, also a lawyer, and no children, I'm pleased to say. I wouldn't bring them in to a toppling world like this. Oh yes, and I never knew my father, which is sad. *C'est finis.*

MUNGO: Maybe you should keep your powder dry until you do have children, which you will.

DAPHNÉ: Don't think you can speak for me.

STEPHEN: [*jumping in*] You're right about the power of words. There's no force greater for working a sea-change on the mind. Maybe I'll speak now. I'm Stephen, a university lecturer in literature and drama.

DAPHNÉ: Okay and what do you bring to the table Stephen?

STEPHEN: I can feedback on our reactions to the situation. My work here is off the page you might say. Yes, we're in a bind, but I can show that it's also an amazing opportunity.

MICHAEL: What do you mean by an opportunity?

STEPHEN: It'll force us to see what we're capable of. We're in a highly charged situation. In my teaching, I've seen how dramatic events uncover our inner sense of theatre. This chasm in nature is liable to unmask us.

MICHAEL: [*practical tone*] Let's hope what's underneath is pleasant then!

MUNGO: Yes, and that the bloated dam up there doesn't spill its guts on us.

STEPHEN: [*jocular*] I also care for my mother part-time. Oh yes, there have been a few girls of course, though I'm officially single again now. Not forever, I hope! [*laughs*]

RUTH: So your mother can still hope for grandchildren?

STEPHEN: [*laughs*] She can hope, if I escape a watery end that is.

MICHAEL: Personally I'm not in to all this self-knowledge. Shall we focus on getting help?

DAPHNÉ: Yes. Let's finish this and call them back.

MUNGO: Okay, who's next up for charades?

RAJ: Yes please, I can tell you my plan, but first I want to tell you about myself, which is very quick and easy.

DAPHNÉ: Come on Raj, what's your story?

RAJ: Yes please. I first came to the UK in the nineteen seventies after the expelling of many people from Uganda under the rule of the terrible dictator, Idi Amin.

MUNGO: Is this a long story?

DAPHNÉ: Ignore him. Carry on Raj.

RAJ: Okay, so I came to Birmingham with my mother. Two years' later I went to assist my brother in West London where he had a small grocery shop. I helped him with his business, and now he has a factory very near to here making sandwiches for many, many Asian grocers across the UK.

MUNGO: [*dry tone*] Ah yes, the sandwiches.

RAJ: Yes that's right. What I can do is to supply food and drink. It's very important, in this case, where we can be trapped for a long while.

MUNGO: Superb, an unvarying diet of Coronation Chicken.

RAJ: Yes and please Mr Mungo, take some now. You must be very hungry! [*he tosses a pack gently to* MUNGO]

MUNGO: For God's sake! [MUNGO *catches the packet and hurls it over the edge of the chasm. The assembled including* MUNGO *fall silent at this demonstration of anger and rejection*]

RAJ: [*looks shocked*] I am now very sorry. I didn't know you were feeling like this.

DAPHNÉ: You're not the one who should be sorry! [*directly to* MUNGO] I'm appalled by your crass behaviour!

MUNGO: Look I just don't want the sandwiches! How many times have I got to say it? It's nothing personal.

MICHAEL: [*angry, but not loud*] It seemed damned personal to me. If I acted like that I'd certainly consider myself a monster!

MUNGO: [*sarcastic tone*] Maybe it's acting that's your problem. You're really quite bad at hiding things.

MICHAEL: [*looks caught-out*] Fuck you Mungo!

MUNGO: [*unmoved, changing tack*] So, how were you brought up, Michael, is it? We're all excited to hear your life story.

MICHAEL: [*recovering his poise*] Okay, yes. I'm a practical person, so my plans would focus on as series of practical steps. First off I'd call the police back to check what's going on. If we can't raise help I'd make plans for spending the night here. Without being too fussy, as we may be picked up in an hour or two.

DAPHNÉ: And your life?

MICHAEL: Yes, okay. I'm a risk assessor. I live with my wife and young son about half an hour from here. I'm trying to source good medical care for him. My work takes me away from home a lot and I was on my way back from a two day work thing. I wish I'd started earlier in the day. I might be home by now.

DAPHNÉ: What's your wife's name?

MICHAEL: Helen, why?

DAPHNÉ: Oh nothing, I just wondered.

STEPHEN: [*pleased to stir*] That's an odd question.

DAPHNÉ: [*cross*] Why? Why is it odd?

STEPHEN: Just because a more obvious question might be to do with his son's health. Asking his wife's name sounds like one woman checking out another. How do you assess that risk Michael? [*laughs*]

DAPHNÉ: I think you're allowing your imagination to run away with you drama guy! We're all strangers here. I'm just being civil. I wouldn't have asked such a personal question without knowing him better.

MICHAEL: [*earnest*] I don't exactly mind discussing my son's condition. I'm trying to raise awareness [*he and DAPHNÉ exchange a look*]

MUNGO: So have we exhausted the playground games now?

[*Before anyone can answer thunder cracks sharply*]

RAJ: Please everyone come to my van. We can shelter from the storm which can be very dangerous! Please, please!

[*All depart except DAPHNÉ and MICHAEL who remain standing at the edge of the collapsed bridge*]

DAPHNÉ: What if the dam does give way? We'll be done for and I'll lose my chance, won't I?

MICHAEL: Sorry, I'm not with you.

DAPHNÉ: You know. Love, a family, children. The usual.

MICHAEL: Is that what you want?

DAPHNÉ: Yes, despite everything.

MICHAEL: It's not what everyone wants. You said so yourself, the world's in a state. I sometimes question bringing Sean in to it.

DAPHNÉ: I know what I said, but people aren't going to stop having children are they?

MICHAEL: I reckon some will.

DAPHNÉ: Perhaps, but isn't the idea to teach them to be part of the solution? Anyway, who else will lead us out of this mess if not our children and their children? I'm going to give up law and do something.

MICHAEL: Something?

DAPHNÉ: Yes, shake the establishment, stir people up. Get change.

MICHAEL: It's a huge commitment? Are you prepared to give your life to it?

DAPHNÉ: Yes, it is a huge commitment, but cometh the hour

cometh the woman right? Besides, if we all wait for someone else to act we're screwed, right?

[*A light rain starts*]

MICHAEL: Here, come under my jacket.

[*They stand very close under* MICHAEL's *jacket*]

DAPHNÉ: What's your view on the climate then? If you have a view.

MICHAEL: [*animated*] Yes I have a view. I think it would be chilling if parents weren't sharing the experience with their children. Sean's doing a project on it at the moment. Loving him connects me to whatever he's doing, at school or wherever.

DAPHNÉ: I wish my father had thought that way.

MICHAEL: How did he think?

DAPHNÉ: I have no idea. As I said earlier he wasn't around to share his thoughts.

MICHAEL: Sorry to hear it. I could never do that to Sean.

DAPHNÉ: Do you believe that one hundred percent? None of us really know ourselves until we're tested. Maybe you haven't been tested. Maybe I haven't either.

MICHAEL: [*stiffly*] I do think I've been tested actually. I can't imagine how going through this nightmare with Sean could have been more of a test.

DAPHNÉ: Maybe, but some of your sex are casual enough on the issue of responsibility.

MICHAEL: [*piqued*] I don't think you can generalise.

DAPHNÉ: Generalisations form opinions, like it or not.

MICHAEL: [*pulling his coat off them*] Clearly we see the world differently.

DAPHNÉ: [*pacifying*] You're too easily offended. I can't escape my own experience, but now I'm talking generally. So, you're the exception, that's great.

MICHAEL:	[*more gently*] Look, when I said we're different it doesn't mean I don't like you. I do. But I have a child, which makes my outlook different from yours.
DAPHNÉ:	[*challenging*] So I can't relate to the calamity the current generation face because I haven't personally conceived?
MICHAEL:	Look, I didn't mean it like that. I simply say that having your own child makes it real. The pain of knowing that they may have a lesser life than you did because of these massive challenges.
DAPHNÉ:	[*frank, to his face*] As it goes Michael, I like you too. I felt that straight off. But you can't claim extra points because of your son, however wonderful he is.
MICHAEL:	That's not what I was saying.
DAPHNÉ:	[*continuing her theme*] It's quite likely all of us, everywhere will face huge turmoil.
MICHAEL:	What do you think will happen?
DAPHNÉ:	Serious environmental events, extremes of weather, maybe not always equal or equivalent, but affecting us all in the end.
MICHAEL:	Can't we build defences?
DAPHNÉ:	Against gradually encroaching sea-level floods, ones affecting entire communities?
MICHAEL:	Have they happened?
DAPHNÉ:	On some islands, yes!
	[*Very loud thunder*]
MICHAEL:	Talking of hell or high water, I think both are on the way!
DAPHNÉ:	Yes, I really hate this. Let's get back to the cars, shall we?

They exit.

ACT 1 SCENE 2

DAPHNÉ *and* MICHAEL *are still on stage alone. The rain has stopped.*
On stage, there an umbrella of Michael's.

MICHAEL: Where were you born?

DAPHNÉ: That's a strange question.

MICHAEL: Why?

DAPHNÉ: Oh just that we're here in this *trés* dodgy situation
                    and you want to know where I was born.

MICHAEL: It's just that you have this very slight French accent,
                    so I wondered if you were born here or there.

DAPHNÉ: Here, though I was schooled in France 'till I was ten.
                    My mother was French and my father's English.

MICHAEL: Was?

DAPHNÉ: Yes, she's dead, but she told me about this place.
                    The house up this road is where my father was born.
                    As you know, he left us when I was a child, and I've
                    never seen his birthplace. That's why I'm here. I'm,
                    well, I was, staying in a local B&B tonight then taking
                    a look around tomorrow.

MICHAEL: I'm sorry about your father. Every child needs a hap-
                    py home life. I suppose you miss him.

DAPHNÉ: You don't miss what you've never had, right?

MICHAEL: [*understanding*] I'm sorry, I didn't mean to pry.

DAPHNÉ: It's okay – all water under the bridge right? [*look at*
                    each other and laugh]

MICHAEL: What bridge?!

DAPHNÉ: Yes! Exactly! Still, there's plenty of water! [*laughs,*
                    then looks back seriously] It's no joke though, is it?
                    Not for anybody.

MICHAEL:	No, I want to believe there's hope though, don't you?
DAPHNÉ:	Yes, but we're not going to be saved by some benign island spirit. It's our choice, and it's right now. There's huge anger in nature. If the torrent over there doesn't get us, the dam up there damned-well will! Look at it. [*motions to the savaged bridge*] We're fiddling with the air-conditioning while Rome topples in flames.
MICHAEL:	Yes. I wish I had a plan.
DAPHNÉ:	Nobody does. [*looks down, thinking*] Anyway, what do you make of that Mungo guy?
MICHAEL:	Him! Obnoxious, right?
DAPHNÉ:	He is, but I know the type. My stepfather's the same. I take it personally, as you can see. I can't stay rational round that attitude, which really pisses me off.
MICHAEL:	He'd piss anyone off!
DAPHNÉ:	Yes, but it's not that simple with me. I feel pissed off at myself. I feel like a child again, angry but safe. He churns me up.
MICHAEL:	You sound as though he has some hold over you.
DAPHNÉ:	Yes, exactly! I guess in some perverse way I view a man like that as a father-figure. It's like I'm frozen in time near him. Bizarre I know, but you can't fight what you feel right?
MICHAEL:	I suppose not. My life's in limbo. Everything revolves around Sean.
DAPHNÉ:	What has he got?
MICHAEL:	[*not ready for this question yet, looks down silently*]
DAPHNÉ:	Okay, tell me when you're ready Michael. [*uses his name a little self-consciously*]
MICHAEL:	Thank you. Have you got kids?
DAPHNÉ:	No! Oh god no! I'd be terrible at it. I'm still too much of a child myself. I've been called quixotic.
MICHAEL:	Which is?

DAPHNÉ:	Idealistic, unrealistic maybe. A bit mad.
MICHAEL:	Having a child changes you. You grow up – you have to.
DAPHNÉ:	[loud *thunder*. DAPHNÉ *and* MICHAEL *move closer*] Jesus! Listen to that! Let's hope I have the chance to grow up! The river's going bananas and the ground's soggy as hell. If we sink it'll be our own stupid fault!
MICHAEL:	Are you frightened?
DAPHNÉ:	[*smiling*] You realise women don't need men to protect them anymore?
MICHAEL:	[*smiles back*] I didn't say it for that reason, but okay, you're on your own then!
DAPHNÉ:	[*again smiling*] Well, perhaps we won't throw the baby out with the bath water. Maybe if the need arises …
	[*more thunder, lightening*]
MICHAEL:	Sure, giving you the best of both worlds.
DAPHNÉ:	[*voice charged by the approaching storm*] Yes, brave new worlds!
MICHAEL:	Aldous Huxley right? I don't know much about literature, but surely his world isn't what we're looking for?
DAPHNÉ:	No?
MICHAEL:	No, it was my GCSE. Huxley imagined a dystopia where humans were mechanically engineered.
DAPHNÉ:	[*animated*] Yes, yes, but I'm thinking of the spell binding story of Shakespeare's *Tempest*. That's my brave new world.
MICHAEL:	Don't know it. I'll have to talk to that drama guy.
DAPHNÉ:	We don't need him. I know it. It's where Miranda meets Ferdinand. He's the first young male she's ever laid eyes on in her life. She's utterly smitten.
MICHAEL:	Oh?

DAPHNÉ:	Yes, I did it at GCSE.
	O wonder! How many goodly creatures are there here! How beauteous mankind is! O brave new world, That has such people in't.
MICHAEL:	Sounds good, though as I say I'm not one for literature.
DAPHNÉ:	[*incredulous*] Good?! Ravishing, magical, bewitching you mean! They're on a magical island. They fall rapturously in love.
MICHAEL:	Right.
DAPHNÉ:	[*laughing, excited*] It helps that he's a prince of course!
MICHAEL:	Ah.
DAPHNÉ:	*Mon Dieu!* Talk about the poetry and the prose!
MICHAEL:	Sorry?
DAPHNÉ:	You English! You could do with a little more romance in the soul!
MICHAEL:	I'm sorry. That ship's already sailed.
DAPHNÉ:	Oh? Will it ever return, or has it been hopelessly shipwrecked? Are there no survivors?
MICHAEL:	[*abashed*] Who knows? ... Anyway you swing wildly between Shakespeare and Huxley don't you?
DAPHNÉ:	[*getting more into her theme, still excited*] Yes! That's right, the poetry and prose. They, we, need each other! We'll need each more as survivors of the storm. If we survive! I'm going to see just what watery grave we're escaping from! [*runs erratically towards the edge of the river*]
MICHAEL:	Christ! Be careful!
	[DAPHNÉ *runs heedlessly towards the edge*]
DAPHNÉ:	Of what exactly?! The end of the world?! Who's being careful of that?!

[*Runs to the very edge,* MICHAEL *alarmed, runs after her catching her arm at brink*]

MICHAEL: Stop this! Are you mad? It could all give way at any moment!

DAPHNÉ: [*excited, wild*] And what difference would it make?!

MICHAEL: [*suddenly piqued*] Don't you care about your life? Don't you have anything to live for?

DAPHNÉ: [*animated*] Oh, perhaps you mean a relationship?

MICHAEL: I'm not sure what I mean. I just think you should stay away from danger.

DAPHNÉ: I'm worth saving you mean?

MICHAEL: Of course you are. We all are. It's like you've popped a pill! Where has all of this come from?

DAPHNÉ: [*defiant*] Why do you ask that? After all, you don't actually know me from Eve do you? We're not all what we seem. In fact very little of what we think is so, is really so.

MICHAEL: Aren't you being rather bleak?

DAPHNÉ: [*wild but lucid*] Am I? Should I be hopeful then? After all, I have a standard quota of Internet 'friends'. I en-joy an antiseptic social-media profile: who I am, where I was born, who I know and where I work. I am not a number! No, I am an icon on a flat-screen. Christ! We're already in Orwell's nightmare! Google, and further ghouls, work tirelessly at neutering us with a joyless inventory of emotions. Happy face, sad face, angry face! Michael, we're heading for extinc-tion by blandness, submitting to the terrifying pied-pipers of the Internet. They're luring us, like lost chil-dren, to the abyss. Instead of raging about even see-ing a future, we're all sending each other pictures of our fucking meals and pets! [*she dares herself closer to the edge*]

MICHAEL: What in hell are you doing?

DAPHNÉ:	[*abandoned*] In hell? Aren't we all at the edge of hell; the inferno that drama guys talks about? I'm doing what we should all do.
MICHAEL:	Which is?
DAPHNÉ:	Do or die!
MICHAEL:	[*fearful and angry*] If you throw yourself in you'll never know if you can 'do', will you?
DAPHNÉ:	It's my choice!
MICHAEL:	[*exasperated and angry*] So throw yourself in then!
DAPHNÉ:	Yeah, wouldn't you like that?
MICHAEL:	It's the absolute last thing I'd want!
DAPHNÉ:	[*searches his face intently for truth, softens*] Okay, I believe you.
MICHAEL:	[*bemused*] Anyway, what can we do about the state of the world?
DAPHNÉ:	[*steps away from the bridge and approaches him earnestly*] Do?! Out of nowhere some random woman, to whom you have no connection, goes nuts at the edge of a chasm scoured out of the earth, probably caused by us, and rages about the state of the planet.
MICHAEL:	Okay.
DAPHNÉ:	So that's what we can do!
MICHAEL:	What?
DAPHNÉ:	Rage! Rage! Each of us in our own way. Go nuts, because going nuts over it is in reality going sane! God! It's probably already too late. People have children. You have a child. What about their chances to live and have children, or simply live out their lives as they wish?!
MICHAEL:	How are you going to mobilise us then, with fear?
DAPHNÉ:	If necessary. What's the alternative? Annihilation can only be avoided by a tempestuous sea-change in our

ways! Common-place monsters control us, wearing grey suits, and talking deceit in reasonable voices. And who buys their snake-oil in pretty bottles? We do!

MICHAEL: Yes, maybe you're right. People don't want to see it though. How are you going to tackle that?

DAPHNÉ: With your help!

MICHAEL: Me?

DAPHNÉ: You or people like you. You don't know yourself. None of us know ourselves until we're made to.

[*Thunder and lightning – The two look at each other intently. Michael walks over and picks up an umbrella from the edge of the stage*]

MICHAEL: Listen, it's going to bucket down again. Let's get the others and call the police back. This has to end soon surely? Come under my umbrella.

DAPHNÉ: [*long pause*] It's everyone's umbrella. Look, I'm sorry I should go. [*Exits*]

ACT 2 SCENE 1

MUNGO *and* MICHAEL *alone on the stage.*

MICHAEL: So you're fucking things up as usual?

MUNGO: Don't know what you mean.

MICHAEL: Yes you do. We're all stranded here, giving you a perfect opportunity to mess with people's minds.

MUNGO: How's Helen?

MICHAEL: Yes, exactly. None of your business Mungo, and Sean even less.

MUNGO: Ah Sean, the fruit of my loins!

MICHAEL: Sean is rid of you once the papers are signed. You're not going back on that are you?

MUNGO: Why would I?

MICHAEL: Because you're untrustworthy. As I said, you play with people. Get their hopes up and then drop them in it. You did that with Sean often enough. Daddy's coming tonight, except that daddy never came.

MUNGO: Maybe it's you that's untrustworthy by being un-trusting. Ever thought of that? I never hurt him intentionally; I have a busy life.

MICHAEL: Yes I know, busy seducing wives.

MUNGO: Don't be a sore loser Michael. At the time, Helen needed a man with balls, I simply provided them.

MICHAEL: Just sign the papers and leave us alone.

MUNGO: So you'll stay with Helen then? After all that's she's put you through?

MICHAEL: I don't have to explain myself to you Mungo. You've done enough damage as it is.

MUNGO: I could do more.

MICHAEL: Don't threaten me or... [*tails off*]

MUNGO: Or what?

MICHAEL: Look, I'm the father in Sean's life. I'm the only one he thinks of as a father. It may not bother you, but it's important to him and to me.

MUNGO: What's your point?

MICHAEL: My point is, once you're out of his life, stay out!

MUNGO: Have no fear, I'll be leaving you to your unremarkable lives; no further involvement. Look, if you've got the papers let's get it done.

MICHAEL: There's no going back you realise?

MUNGO: I never go back Michael, that's my strength. What's yours?

MICHAEL: Attempting to be a half decent human-being is all I aim for. Here. [*passes a document to* MUNGO *who scribbles his signature*]

MUNGO: Done.

MICHAEL: Yes. Now I have to go.

MUNGO: You've got your eye on that French girl I see. I'd tread carefully there if I were you. She's too much for you to handle. Just like Helen, too spirited. Interesting genes, I imagine.

MICHAEL: Really? And what's your angle Mungo? She's certainly not your type; unmarried. Anyway, as I say, I've got to go. I hope once we're out of here I never want to see you again.

MUNGO: It's a promise.

[MICHAEL *exits, some moments later* DAPHNÉ *enters.*]

DAPHNÉ: Is Michael around?

MUNGO: He just left. You seem very keen to see him.

DAPHNÉ: I didn't say that. I want to talk to him that's all.

MUNGO: [dry rather than sarcastic] Yes, of course, he's a nice guy, Michael. Only he'll never be anything. He lacks the instinct for success.

DAPHNÉ: [dismissive] I don't know why you're saying this. I have no angle on anything or anyone here. None of us even know each other.

MUNGO: Not yet, no.

DAPHNÉ: Not yet? I thought you were going to forget us all instantly?

MUNGO: True, but when I like a person, I endeavour to get to know them better.

DAPHNÉ: So I'm an exception? Does that mean what I think it means?

MUNGO: I don't know what you think. The point is I can do people some good if I like them.

DAPHNÉ: Oh yes? How's that?

MUNGO: Well, let's say you wanted to move on from your current law firm to the foremost firm in the UK. How would that sound?

DAPHNÉ: [falls silent for some seconds] So how would that work?

MUNGO: I know people. I have influence, power if you like.

DAPHNÉ: And if I were to 'like' what would the terms of our agreement be? Does it by any chance involve a hotel room?

MUNGO: We don't know yet what it would amount to. You interest me. You give out signals most people keep hidden. I observe them in you.

DAPHNÉ: I don't know what you mean.

DAPHNÉ: You're daring. Your character suggests you might be open to gainful opportunities.

DAPHNÉ:	Gainful? That sounds like a euphemism if ever I heard one! What are they, these gainful opportunities?
MUNGO:	Ambition, monetary advantage, experience.
DAPHNÉ:	You mean I'd be easily seduced by power and sleep with you?
MUNGO:	You'd do nothing easily, that I'm clear on, and I don't seek to introduce power as a thing here.
DAPHNÉ:	Power's always a thing Mungo!
MUNGO:	Right! And right there is the true person.
DAPHNÉ:	Meaning what exactly?
MUNGO:	Meaning you're open for business. That somewhere in you, in your fiery core there are both doubts and possibilities.
DAPHNÉ:	Possibilities of what?
MUNGO:	Possibilities that you can go further; that you can do better than that guy Michael.
DAPHNÉ:	[angry, rattled] Michael's a decent man. He's got a conscience. You wouldn't know what that is of course, so it's pointless having this conversation. Jesus Christ Mungo! I can't listen to any more of your bullshit! [exits]

ACT 2 SCENE 2

DAPHNÉ, MICHAEL, RAJ, MUNGO and STEPHEN.

MUNGO: Christ alive! Where have the bloody plod got to?

STEPHEN: Don't know. Maybe you can call pull a few strings?

MUNGO: I can pull yours if you like?

STEPHEN: To dance to your tune? You'd like that.

MUNGO: I'd 'like' to be out of this water-logged playpen.

STEPHEN: As would we all, but we'll have to wait it out. We're all pissed off, but what can we do?

MUNGO: What we can do is, gather up the other odds and sods stuck in this misadventure and walk to the nearest village. Enlist the aid of some yokels, who can help us out for a couple of farthings and distant promise of a ride in my car.

STEPHEN: A wonderful tableau! You can be an upper-crust nob-head, while we stand around grovelling.

MUNGO: Haven't you got some aimless drama to act out?

RAJ: [*worried*] Mr Mungo, you cannot walk from here to anywhere. The police say it is very dangerous. Mr Michael has just been talking to them on his telephone and they are very clear on this point.

MUNGO: I don't need advice thank you. I'm not a six year old.

DAPHNÉ: Even if you behave like one?

MUNGO: [*pitying*] You know you're attractive but unrealistic; an *ingénue.*

DAPHNÉ: I don't want you to be attracted to me thanks.

MUNGO: I didn't say I was actually. Though I'd forgotten how we're sanitising all drives and appetites these days. Only I haven't signed that particular contract.

RAJ:	Mr Mungo, please, a true gentleman never talks this way to a lady.
DAPHNÉ:	Thank you Raj, but you won't get any change out of a man like that.
MUNGO:	[*sarcastic*] Oh of course, I'm an animal. But, breaking news, we all are!
MICHAEL:	[*irritated*] I'm sorry to spoil this game but I think we should be asking ourselves how we get out of this rattrap.
MUNGO:	I don't see anyone stopping you getting us out.
MICHAEL:	I'll call the police again.
RAJ:	Yes, you should do that Mr Michael. We could be in real trouble.
DAPHNÉ:	I'll call.
MUNGO:	Oh for Christ's sake, how many grown adults does it take to use a phone?
DAPHNÉ:	Shut up Mungo! There's been no signal. I'm trying again now. [*dials, frustrated*] Still no signal! Shit!
STEPHEN:	Why don't we explore a little further round here? We can spread out, take a look around.
RAJ:	I am very worried that someone may come to harm. Should we not stay together?
MICHAEL:	[*impatient*] Look, all this talk is getting us nowhere! You stay here while I take a look around. Give me five minutes. [*he leaves*]
STEPHEN:	[*laughing*]. And then there were nine!
DAPHNÉ:	[*angry*].You can shut up too!
STEPHEN:	Oh come on! I'm just trying to lighten the mood!
RAJ:	It's not a matter for joking Mr Stephen. I am really concerned about the safety of all of us, especially for Mr Michael now he has gone. If the dam we have all heard about is ready to break, we are all in very great danger. The weather in the whole world is very

strange nowadays. In India the times of the monsoons have all changed, and water now rises up very high in some villages.

MUNGO: We don't need anecdotes from half-way across the world to tell us about the weather here in Devon do we?

DAPHNÉ: [angry] Yes we do! That's the whole point. What we do in one place affects another. I'd have thought an educated man would be aware of that!

MUNGO: Yes? Well the whole thing's utterly unproven.

DAPHNÉ: What is?

MUNGO: Climate change. I don't see a problem.

DAPHNÉ: The problem 'is' not seeing a problem. Just as it is those who think only in the singular; people who deliver their viewpoints from their fortresses. Do you really think you can't be touched by the world outside your walls?

MUNGO: So I'm to blame because I don't automatically buy every crack-brained theory I read?

DAPHNÉ: It's science, not a story-line. It'll get you too. Not simply because you deserve it, but because, inconveniently, everyone is in the firing line.

MUNGO: I don't accept it.

DAPHNÉ: That's because you don't recognise other people's existence. God! You're a one-man Grand Central Station from which all trains of thought arrive and depart.

MUNGO: I've never been a team player if that's what you mean.

DAPHNÉ: [angrily] That would be all very well if we were talking about a bank. But this isn't a matter of profits going up or down! This is people living or dying! People are already dying because of the greed of people who think solely of themselves. Damnit, we're lost!

RAJ:	[*earnestly, without rancour*]. She is very correct. And at this moment I hope Mr Michael is not in danger. It is quite true Mr Mungo, what Miss Daphné says. We must think of everyone. In life we need the other person's help.
MUNGO:	[*dismissive*] I can't think how I'd need help from any of you.
STEPHEN:	Like I said, your outlook will be your undoing. You've heard of poetic justice, haven't you?
MUNGO:	I'm not superstitious and I don't credit hippies with over much brain power. I've done nothing wrong. I'm simply living my life.
DAPHNÉ:	That's a crap argument! You're living comfortably only because, for now, you're not affected by your casual selfishness.
RAJ:	As I say, I am now really worried about Mr Michael. Shall we not call the police again and tell them what has happened?
STEPHEN:	[*laughs*] Yes, he could be lying at the bottom of a ravine right now!
RAJ:	That is not a nice thing to say Mr Stephen.
STEPHEN:	Okay, I'm sorry, I feel the onset of chaos that's all. I'm simply a conduit, it's nothing personal. I want him to be okay just like the rest of you. Or, [*adopting RAJ's phraseology*] maybe not quite as much as Miss Daphné wants Mr Michael to make it!
DAPHNÉ:	[*derisively*] You think yourself clever don't you?
STEPHEN:	Not especially, but you really shouldn't take offence so easily. No tragedy has actually occurred, has it?
DAPHNÉ:	Who knows? It may have, and if it has, or does, we know your take on it, don't we?
STEPHEN:	Oh please not melodrama! It's a poor relation to real drama!

MUNGO:	Farce is nearer the mark! Goodbye asylum, I'm off to see for myself. [*exits*]
DAPHNÉ:	[*tries her mobile again*] Still no signal! [*exclaims as* MICHAEL *reappears*] Where in Christ's name have you been?
RAJ:	[*extremely pleased*] Oh Mr Michael! Thanks to God you are alright!
MICHAEL:	I've been as far as I can safely, but there's no sign of anyone! The road's empty for miles. Anyway there's been no rain for some time now so perhaps any stragglers have made it to safety.
RAJ:	Let us hope so Mr Michael. I for one will be very happy when this terrible night is over.
MICHAEL:	Yes, I'm worried about what's going on at home. If we can't get out of this soon I'm thinking of walking up as far as the cutting. Maybe the police and rescue are coming that way. I can't get a signal on my phone.
DAPHNÉ:	Nobody can.
STEPHEN:	[*looking from* MICHAEL *to* DAPHNÉ] If Miranda and Ferdinand are ever to wed we'll have to find a way out of here. If this follows the story, it will all turn out to be a dream, and you'll live happily ever after!
MICHAEL:	There's no denying Mungo is a piece of work, but he was right about you. Your brain's wasted from years of pot and one-night stands.
STEPHEN:	That's where you've got me wrong. I observe. That's my thing.
DAPHNÉ:	Sounds pretty calculating. So you don't take part, you simply wait to see what happens to the rest of us. A kind of experiment?
MICHAEL:	Weren't you going on about the Uncommitted in Dante's hell earlier? Aren't you lined-up for eternal torment for not choosing?

STEPHEN:	Oh that. It's just a work of fiction of course.
MICHAEL:	Maybe, but the line between fact and fiction can get blurred.
STEPHEN:	It is blurred. Life's blurred.
MICHAEL:	So who can we trust in this fog?
STEPHEN:	Okay, forget Dante, which is a bit grim. Like I just said, you're both better cast in *The Tempest*. You two have great parts full of steamy promise and everything works out great in the end. Everyone's saved and all is forgiven.
MICHAEL:	You seem to have invented a whole fantasy for us. We don't know each other any more than we know you.
DAPHNÉ:	[*pause, softly*] Is it so far-fetched?
MICHAEL:	[*surprised*] Sorry?
DAPHNÉ:	Two humans thrown together by fate?
STEPHEN:	See! Okay, I'll leave you to it. [*exits*]
MICHAEL:	[*tentative*] I'm sorry if ...
DAPHNÉ:	[*anxious to explain*] No, no don't apologise. It's me. I'm beginning to question what I say or think in the middle of all this turmoil. It's exciting in a weird way. It's like being carried along by the flood, not knowing where you're going to end up, danger all around us.
MICHAEL:	Yes, I get it, and I feel it too. I'm not in a good place in my life. Things are unsettled. My marriage is rocky to say the least.
DAPHNÉ:	Not your *grand amour*?
MICHAEL:	Afraid not, you?
DAPHNÉ:	No, but I like him.
MICHAEL:	Is that enough?
DAPHNÉ:	Probably not. [*they walk to the edge of the river, staying close*] So we're the Uncommitted in the inferno of love?

MICHAEL: I guess. [*move closer, looking to see they're not observed. Long kiss*] ... I'm sorry, I...

DAPHNÉ: Sssshhh – Don't spoil it. Spontaneous is good. It's what you really feel, even if it's just at that second. [*they kiss again. Longish pause*] There was something I wanted to ask you.

MICHAEL: [*hesitant*] Okay?

DAPHNÉ: What was Mungo talking about when he said you were acting?

MICHAEL: [*nervous, long pause, eventually*] Okay the truth. I actually don't have a child of my own.

DAPHNÉ: [*shocked*] So who's Sean? You made him up? Anyway, how would Mungo know any of this?

MICHAEL: [*ploughing ahead*] Look Sean is completely real; it's just that he's not mine exactly.

DAPHNÉ: Not exactly? Then who is he?

MICHAEL: He's Helen's child by another man. I feel absolutely that he's mine. His is mine. I love him and I look after him.

DAPHNÉ: But how would Mungo know this?

MICHAEL: [*deep breath*] Because he's the father.

DAPHNÉ: The father!? Michael you've got to be kidding?! You didn't seem to know each other. You would have acted differently around him surely if he's the father?

MICHAEL: We have an agreement not to give that away. We were driving this way to meet up in layby a few miles up the road. We've been here before. We're going through a process of adoption, and we have to sign paperwork. He's an uncaring shit and I love Sean, so I'm adopting him. The school have to report too.

DAPHNÉ: [*approving*] That's wonderful Michael. If you love him as you say you're doing exactly the right thing.

~46~

	You're taking responsibility for something beyond yourself. We need more people like you.
MICHAEL:	Maybe, but until the adoption is complete he's got a hold over me.
DAPHNÉ:	Yes. You need to go easy. You could have blown it with some of the things you said.
MICHAEL:	I know.
DAPHNÉ:	He's pretty old to be the father of a seven year old isn't he?
MICHAEL:	Yes. She got to know him through work. She's in finance. He got in to her mind, with all his spiel about money and status. He's estranged from his own grown-up children because they couldn't stomach his habits.
DAPHNÉ:	And what about Helen? If she's been unfaithful will you stay with her?
MICHAEL:	No, I've been waiting for the right moment. We moved recently and Sean needs to be settled at his new school before we do anything. I'm spending all my free time looking for treatment. I'm hoping he'll be okay, if I can just find the right medics.
	[A loud argument interrupts them. MUNGO enters pursued by a youth on a foot scooter]
MUNGO:	Get this little shit away from me!
YOUTH:	I'll kill you man!

ACT 2 SCENE 3

MUNGO, RAJ, MICHAEL, DAPHNÉ, STEPHEN and YOUTH

YOUTH: Take it back man! Give me respect or I'll mess you up! [*wild, angry, throws down his scooter, chases* MUNGO]

STEPHEN: [*laughing*] It's a wild-eyed monster chasing the court jester!

MUNGO: [*standing at arm's length from the youth with a rolled umbrella outstretched for protection*] Shut up hippy. Someone get this gangster away from me! Anyone?! Surely we can help each other out here?

YOUTH: He says my tattoos are vulgar innit!

MUNGO: Yes, absolutely so. They're tantamount to self-mutilation. He was sniffing round my car. These people are all car thieves. He's in a gang that steals and sells high value cars to order.

DAPHNÉ: What!? Are you mad? What evidence do you have?

[*more lunging*]

RAJ: Oh my heavens. Can you please both be calm? Someone can be hurt very badly.

YOUTH: [*goes for* MUNGO *again and continues to do so periodically*] I told you, I'm gonna mess you up!

MUNGO: Look, can't someone do something?! My life's in danger here!

DAPHNÉ: Now you want our help? You mean people may actually need each other? Weren't you just saying you couldn't see how you'd need any of us?

MUNGO: This is different. Can't you see this nutjob wants my
            blood!?

MICHAEL: What happened? Why does he want your blood
            Mungo?

YOUTH: He disrespected me man! He says people don't want
            my type around.

MUNGO: What I actually said was to go away because I found
            his look offensive.

DAPHNÉ: Oh that's much better, isn't it? You really are a dick,
            Mungo. What convinces you you're so much better
            than other people?

MUNGO: I can count to ten and spell my own name!

RAJ: [interjecting] Look I'm very sorry for what you have
            suffered young man, but please stop fighting. Mr
            Mungo didn't mean what he said, I'm sure.

MUNGO: I meant every word! Look what this country has de-
            scended to! Street gangs speaking empty patois!

STEPHEN: [to the YOUTH] Apart from what he's saying now,
            how did he show you disrespect?

YOUTH: [still lunging] I was on a bus when the flood forced us
            to stop. I got separated and walked down here.
            When I saw all these cars I thought I could help man.
            I was looking at the car, just looking!

MUNGO: You see! He was prospecting!

YOUTH: Then this dick comes along. He tells me I ain't no use
            to nobody on a scooter, unless it's a water-scooter.
            He says I should go back to my drug gang. I just
            wanted to help. He's a dick, man!

RAJ: [alarmed] Please, please don't be angry anymore. I
            have some sandwiches for you and also something
            to drink. Look. [RAJ holds them up. The YOUTH seems
            more pacified. MUNGO runs, reaching the edge. The
            YOUTH runs after him]

MUNGO: Get back! I'll fall you fool!

YOUTH:	I said I'd kill you! [*runs at* MUNGO*, who steps aside at the last moment.* YOUTH *goes over the edge*]
	[*Stunned silence for some long seconds*]
STEPHEN:	Holy shit, you've really done it now, Mungo!
MUNGO:	Christ! Oh Christ! Why...
RAJ:	Oh heavens Mr Mungo. This is very awful and very serious. What can we all do?
STEPHEN:	All? He's on his own as far as I'm concerned. I know what I saw and it doesn't look good!
RAJ:	I think we must all stick together. I think it was a terrible accident. Does everyone agree with me?
MUNGO:	He's right. This guy, ah ... Raj, he's right! He's got excellent judgement I've always said.
DAPHNÉ:	No, you've always cursed him for offering you straightforward kindness. Anyway I don't think it's that simple. Someone has just died.
MUNGO:	He might not have died! He went in, but perhaps he got ashore further down the river!
RAJ:	Let's all pray that Mr Mungo is correct.
DAPHNÉ:	Your optimism is heart-warming Mungo, but it's clearly only out of concern for your own skin.
MICHAEL:	Why were you being such a dick to the guy Mungo? Did it make you feel better about yourself to put the youth down?
MUNGO:	I can't stand vulgarity. The guy was uneducated. I couldn't understand him. He was speaking another language.
STEPHEN:	Yes, the language of youth. You should try getting down with the kids Mungo. It would do you good!
MUNGO:	[*recovering some poise*] Haven't you got some drugs to take?
STEPHEN:	Haven't you got someone to go shine your terrifyingly shiny car?

MUNGO:	What the hell are you talking about?
STEPHEN:	I simply wonder how some people manage never to accumulate the shit off the road we all travel.
MUNGO:	I have people, so what? So would you, if you had the means.
DAPHNÉ:	Don't compare people with yourself.
MICHAEL:	We're wasting time. There's been a death and probably a crime. We should try the police again.
STEPHEN:	A whodunit, fab!
MUNGO:	Keep your nineteen-sixty-four-speak to yourself. There's no whodunit here. The guy was clearly unhinged. He brought this on himself.
STEPHEN:	Yeah right! I'm not sure the police will see it that way!
MICHAEL:	I'm calling.
MUNGO:	I'm not admitting to anything. I'm the victim here. By rights I should sue the family for attempted murder.
MICHAEL:	Hello? [*signals surprise to the others that he's got through*] Yes, police please? [*pause*] I'm on the B1077 near Little Millbridge, near the bridge itself. Yes thank you. [*pause*] Yes my name's Michael Gould. [*pause*] Thank you. Hello, police? Okay yes, I want to report a crime. [*pause*] A death.
MUNGO:	[*angry*] You don't know that!
MICHAEL:	[*turns away from MUNGO's interruption*] Yes. Well a youth, I'm afraid I don't know his name, has gone in to the river at a collapsed bridge. He must have died. We're cut off here, you may know?
MUNGO:	You're prejudicing my case dammit! I was side stepping a vicious attack by a known criminal.
MICHAEL:	Yes I'll be on this number, thank you. [*ends call*] They'll call back.

DAPHNÉ:	[*to* MUNGO] A known criminal? Are you mad? You don't know anything about that poor kid. You don't know and you don't care. What you've done will affect Christ knows how many other people. Have you even considered that? No, Mungo! Saving your own skin is the only issue. You disgust me!
MUNGO:	I don't know what you mean. I didn't do anything.
DAPHNÉ:	Sure. We all witnessed what happened. The truth hasn't dawned on you, has it?
MUNGO:	[*long pause, silent and shocked*] I can't have done ... I didn't know that would happen. I'm not guilty ... I don't understand...
	[*Violent thunder sounds*]
RAJ:	This is so terrible. The dam will be under even more pressure now. Let us all find some shelter.

They move off towards the cars.

ACT 3 SCENE 1

MUNGO DAPHNÉ, MICHAEL, RAJ, and STEPHEN.

MUNGO's *look has changed to one of desperate realisation.*

STEPHEN:	The youth is dead Mungo.
MUNGO:	[*wailing*] I didn't kill him!
STEPHEN:	It was always coming.
MUNGO:	I didn't kill him! It was an accident, or suicide.
STEPHEN:	[*sarcastic*] Of course it was.
MUNGO:	[*desperate but defiant*] Christ, this is a plot. You're all trying to trick me in to admitting something I didn't do! The guy did it himself! We all saw that! You all saw it!
RAJ:	[*calm*] I saw what it was Mr Mungo. I'm asking myself what to think. The youth is dead and that is terrible.
STEPHEN:	The youth is dead! Long live the youth!
MICHAEL:	[*to STEPHEN, angry*] There's something wrong with you. Someone's died! Don't you get that!? [STEPHEN *shrugs*]
DAPHNÉ:	[*putting a hand on his arm*] Michael, leave him. He's just an observer remember? Anyway, something must be done.
MUNGO:	[*shouting*] No! No! You heard what the guy said. He said he was going to kill me! He did try to kill me. Everyone heard that, didn't they? If he went over the edge, it was his own fault for trying to destroy me!
STEPHEN:	It's game over Mungo. It can't be reversed. It was your choice, even if you didn't actually push him it

	amounts to the same thing. He's lost because you didn't care to stop it.
MUNGO:	This is insane. You sound like some kind of jumped-up prophet. Who are you to judge me? I'll quite happily face a real judge, thank you. It's all a mad dream.
STEPHEN:	A dream with a dead body. What have you got against the young, Mungo?
MUNGO:	[*pleading*] I like the young. I've got children. I've got a daughter who I haven't seen since she was a baby, but she's still dear to me.
STEPHEN:	He's wandering in the mind. Who is this missing daughter?
MUNGO:	She was born near here, like all our family. She's grown up. I'm sure she's made something of herself.
DAPHNÉ:	[*wondering voice*] Near here?
MUNGO:	Yes, we're all from here. Look I want to get back to civilisation and talk to my lawyer. This can all be sorted out without the need for a hearing. I won't be put in the stocks because of some transient. This is a travesty. I'm a rich man. I have more influence than you people know.
STEPHEN:	[*laughing*] Now he's *Citizen* bloody *Cane*! You're hiding from the truth Mungo, old chap!
MUNGO:	[*angry*] I'm going to the van to phone my lawyer. I can't think straight with all this double-talk. [*leaves*]
RAJ:	Please wait. I will open the van for you Mr Mungo. [RAJ *follows*]
MICHAEL:	[*to* STEPHEN] And you Stephen? What kind of man are you? Single, freewheeling and uncommitted? Are you hiding from the truth? A man with no responsibilities and no sense of responsibility? If anything you're worse than Mungo. You don't care about anything do you, not people or place?
STEPHEN:	Oh come on boys and girls! Play the game!

DAPHNÉ:	[*coming out of her reverie*] No! You play the game! You want to feel excitement and drama, but never at your own expense. What about a world in total melt-down, Stephen? Would that be exciting enough for you? Do you think sitting on the fence will delay the inevitable? Is the peril of the planet not exciting enough for you? When will you pick a side?
STEPHEN:	Jesus! You're one scary woman!
DAPHNÉ:	You mean I've worked you out?
STEPHEN:	[*deflecting*] You realise, he just wants to jump your bones, don't you?
MICHAEL:	Is that what you said in the sixties?
STEPHEN:	[*to* DAPHNÉ] It's never more than two seconds from a man's mind, you know?
MICHAEL:	By that I suppose you mean sex, woman? If so, then yes of course I think of them. I'm young, it's natural. I hope I channel it differently from you though. In your tone of detachment you imply women are just further drama without consequences.
STEPHEN:	Is this psychoanalysis free?
DAPHNÉ:	Aren't you a bit 'out of time'?
STEPHEN:	Good song! I'm surprised you know it.
DAPHNÉ:	I had a stepfather who was out of time too. There's nothing new about you, Stephen. I know you too well, or men like you.
STEPHEN:	Are we going to stand for that Mickey baby?
MICHAEL:	For what?
STEPHEN:	The future is female! All that!
DAPHNÉ:	You're pathetic, Stephen. Michael's a grown-up, maybe he gets it.
MICHAEL:	[*facing her*] I don't say I agree with that slogan.
STEPHEN:	Oops, trouble in paradise?

DAPHNÉ:	Shut up Stephen! [STEPHEN *gestures zipping his mouth*]
MICHAEL:	[*continuing his train of thought*] For me that sounds war-like. I don't think the future is female any more than it's male. I hope the future is balanced. That it's human. What should I tell my son? That he's a poor relation to the girl next door? Are mothers of sons expected to support that?
STEPHEN:	Well, there we have it! The world according to Mickey! That sure told her!
DAPHNÉ:	Yes! It told me there are reasoning minds trying to span the chasm of views. Why don't you dare yourself to look over the edge Stephen? Do you think that what you'll see there will destroy you? You need to decide what side you're on; the destroyers or the saviours. But above all, decide. Until we know the teams, we can't play the game.
STEPHEN:	Games, dreams. Surely this small piece of soggy magic is about ready to dissolve. As I'm going to now dissolve to answer a functional demand. I reckon this is dear old Prospero's 'baseless fabric of a vision', and all of us, ready for our curtain call. [*exits*]
DAPHNÉ:	[*quiet, thoughtful*] It's bloody strange.
MICHAEL:	What is? You look as if you've seen a ghost.
DAPHNÉ:	Maybe I have.
MICHAEL:	What do you mean?
DAPHNÉ:	Didn't you hear what Mungo said?
MICHAEL:	That he wasn't guilty. It's what he always says. He's a schmuck.
DAPHNÉ:	No not that. You can't have heard it.
MICHAEL:	Okay, what did he say that I didn't hear?
DAPHNÉ:	About having a daughter that he hadn't seen for years.
MICHAEL:	Yes, I think I heard that. What of it?

DAPHNÉ:	[*looks at him intently*] A daughter Michael. He has a daughter.
MICHAEL:	[*light dawns*] Oh my Christ! You mean …
DAPHNÉ:	Yes, that's what I mean. It all fits.
MICHAEL:	But hold on it can't be so.
DAPHNÉ:	Why not?
MICHAEL:	Because you'd have known who he was when he did his pompous bio. He said his name. Mungo De Fren.
DAPHNÉ:	That's easy. My mother would never give me a name. She thought when I was old enough I'd go after him and get hurt.
MICHAEL:	But you could have researched. These days it's easier than it used to be to get that information.
DAPHNÉ:	Yes, the huge irony is that that's exactly what I was doing. This was stage one, see where he was born.
MICHAEL:	Jesus I see what you mean.
DAPHNÉ:	And you know the really sad part?
MICHAEL:	Isn't it all sad?
DAPHNÉ:	Yes, but the saddest part is that he's just like my stepfather, only worse.
MICHAEL:	Right. You'd hoped for something better?
DAPHNÉ:	Yes, I've always imagined him as a good man; a kind man. But in the end he's just Mungo. A selfish womaniser. Any woman, even one young enough to be his daughter. Even me, Michael, without knowing it!
MICHAEL:	[*trying to help*] Bright though. I know him well enough to assure you of that.
DAPHNÉ:	And more terrifying still, I can see myself in him. Character doesn't go by gender. I've been just as ruthless in my work sometimes. I even have considered, just for a second, taking help from him to get on. It's in the genes.

MICHAEL:	So are you looking for someone who's made their mark in the world, as he put it? A winner?
DAPHNÉ:	Yes, that was spooky fatherly advice wasn't it? And the answer is yes, I am, but not in the way he means. I'm looking for someone with basic humanity. [*pause, between humour and sober*] What's your profile like Michael?
MICHAEL:	[*gentle laugh*] Am I under investigation?
DAPHNÉ:	[*smiles*] I'm not the police.
MICHAEL:	Shame, we might be out of this mess by now if you were.
DAPHNÉ:	[*more serious*] What do you think will happen to Mungo?
MICHAEL:	I don't know. It could be argued he simply stepped aside to save himself.
DAPHNÉ:	I promise you, in the law anything can be argued. It's a game.
MICHAEL:	Yes, but I wouldn't want to make that call. He's a self-centred shit, but I prefer him to the flower-power guy.
DAPHNÉ:	Me too. There's something so untouchable about that man. It's like he froze over at some point, trapping all his real feelings under the ice, a kind of human glacier passing among the warm-blooded.
MICHAEL:	[*smiles, ironic*] You're warm-blooded enough for all of us!
DAPHNÉ:	[*laughs*] Yes, I suppose you're right there. [*brief pause*] I'm pleased you're no man of ice though. [*she kisses him lightly on the cheek*]

ACT 3 SCENE 2

MICHAEL DAPHNÉ MUNGO RAJ

MICHAEL: The police say they should be with us within the hour.

MUNGO: [*bitter*] I suppose you'll all betray me?

DAPHNÉ: You're not worth the thirty pieces of silver Mungo. We'll simply report what happened. Would that bother you?

MUNGO: It's what you think happened that bothers me. I know what happened!

RAJ: I hope that the police realise it has been a very difficult situation for us all. I don't think Mr Mungo really wanted to hurt anyone.

DAPHNÉ: That, Raj, is because you look only for the good in people.

RAJ: There *is* good in everyone. It is not just for this I say it though. Mr Mungo is just as he is. You cannot make a tiger in to a lion.

MICHAEL: Unless of course you paint over its spots! Mungo certainly isn't beyond that!

MUNGO: Listen to what Raj is saying! He knows me. He knows I wouldn't deliberately cause someone's death!

RAJ: [*calm, gentle*] Actually Mr Mungo I don't know you, but I know people like you. You are a weak and selfish man who likes to think only of himself. I don't think you are a truly wicked man. However you should now show that you're truly sorry for what happened.

MUNGO: [*bristling slightly*] Maybe you don't fully understand what happened.

RAJ: Forgive me Mr Mungo, but I think I understand very well. You met this young man on the road and you immediately thought badly of him. He had many tattoos, and he wasn't an educated man. In your mind, this made him less than you. That is why you said things to him that made him very angry. For that, you should be sorry.

MUNGO: He was a peasant! How can one possibly relate to someone who doesn't speak your language?

DAPHNÉ: Is that what you really think? He might have saved your worthless skin had the situation taken a different turn. He came here to help.

MICHAEL: What's your defence then Mungo? What's your line when the police arrive to take you away? How will you plead?

DAPHNÉ: He'll plead pompous arsehole, won't you Mungo? Then some smart, highly paid lawyer will get you off because of lack of evidence. That's it isn't it? You'll reject your responsibilities as you have all your life.

MUNGO: I don't know what you mean. What do you know about my life?

DAPHNÉ: Enough.

MUNGO: I didn't mean to kill the guy. You all know that.

MICHAEL: Even if we agree with you they could still quite easily go for manslaughter, and we were all witnesses. We can testify.

MUNGO: [*grappling with his emotions*] Look, look … I swear I didn't mean for this to happen. I didn't mean for that youth to die, if he is dead. I had an argument with him, but it didn't end as expected. I thought he'd just go away.

DAPHNÉ: Because for you, things do just *go away*. Once money and influence have cleansed your hands, you divert the stream of pain in to other lives.

MUNGO: [*sounds distraught, contrite*] Okay. I was wrong! I shouldn't have started on that guy! I see that he was only trying to help. I made a mistake! We all make mistakes, don't we?

DAPHNÉ: Like me you mean?

MUNGO: [*puzzled*] You?

DAPHNÉ: Yes, like me. I was driving this way to see my father's birth-place, when the storm hit us. It turned out it was a storm bringing a deluge of truths.

MUNGO: [*very slowly the truth dawning*] But, surely not, not you.

DAPHNÉ: Me.

MUNGO: You.

MICHAEL: You talk about us all making mistakes Mungo. That's true enough. But [*reaching out a hand to* DAPHNÉ] here's a mistake you can't buy off. [*long pause, as all digest the facts*]

RAJ: [*finally*] Look I'm sure everyone must all be hungry now. I have more food here with me. [*he gets a bag and starts passing round more sandwiches. Eventually he comes to* MUNGO. *Hesitating slightly he reaches out with the package.* MUNGO *looks abashed and slowly accepts the food*]

MUNGO: [*quietly*] Thank you.

STEPHEN: [*enters cheerful, accompanied by a police-woman*] Look what the cat dragged in!

POLICE-WOMAN: Can I ask you all to listen carefully please. I need to know if there is a Mungo De Fren present.

MUNGO: [*Simply*] I am he.

POLICE-WOMAN: Okay, good. We've assessed the ground as safe, though the dam is still in a critical condition, so we

	need to be quick. I'll need you all to make your way down past the vehicles to the cutting. You'll be collected from there and taken to the local community hall, where you will be processed. Those of you who are considered fit and well will then be able to make your onward journeys. Mr de Fren?
MUNGO:	Yes?
POLICE-WOMAN:	I'll need you to come with me. A man was pulled from the river a few hundred yards down-stream. I understand you may have further information? We'll be contacting the rest of you on this matter too, so if you could please leave your contact details at the meeting point. Thank you.
MUNGO:	[*with dread*] Is he ...
POLICE-WOMAN:	[*cutting him off*] I can't discuss the matter here I'm afraid Mr De Fren. We'll go in to it fully at the station. [*they exit along with* RAJ]
STEPHEN:	[*still cheerful*] All's well that ends well!
DAPHNÉ:	I guess that depends on your definition of well.
MICHAEL:	And ends.
STEPHEN:	I think it's a wrap myself! [*laughing*] Anyway, nice to meet you both, have fun! [*exits*]
MICHAEL:	Madman!
DAPHNÉ:	Worse Michael, a sane man without feeling.
MICHAEL:	I don't know how you've managed to stay so rational.
DAPHNÉ:	I know. But the experience has changed me. I felt freed in my mind confronting Mungo. And meeting you, well ... [*falls silent*]
MICHAEL:	Well, for me it's been a revelation ... [*falls silent*]
DAPHNÉ:	[*approaches, hold his face in her hands*] Yes, me too.
MICHAEL:	[*pause to smile and respond*] What will you do?
DAPHNÉ:	Save our boat from the storm.

MICHAEL:	On your own?
DAPHNÉ:	I hope with you, and people like you.
MICHAEL:	It's a very large boat to save.
DAPHNÉ:	It's the only one we've got. We have no choice. We're not going to stand by while it sinks forever are we?
MICHAEL:	I have my child to consider. I have to see to him.
DAPHNÉ:	I know, and you will. We will.
MICHAEL:	We?
DAPHNÉ:	Your life and my life are a tiny part of a huge picture. But it is one picture. This is about everything and everyone. [*quotes*] The great globe itself, ye all that it inherit...
MICHAEL:	We've been through our own tempest, right?
DAPHNÉ:	Only a minor one. I fear there will be many more and worse to come. We've found each other in the muddle, but we need more help. As we speak, extreme weather wracks pretty much every part of the world. Standing together may give us a chance, but things are serious and largely unknown.
MICHAEL:	[*pause as he absorbs this*] Shall we walk up to the cutting together?
DAPHNÉ:	Yes, and let's do more than that! [*exit*]
END	